Welcome to
The Giggle Club

The Giggle Club is a collection of picture books made to put a giggle into early reading. There are funny stories about a contrary mouse, a dancing fox, a turtle with a trumpet, a pig with a ball, a hungry monster, a wide-mouthed frog, an elephant who sneezes away the jungle and lots more! Each of these characters is a member of **The Giggle Club**, but anyone can join: just pick up a **Giggle Club** book, read it and get giggling!

Turn to the checklist on the inside back cover and check off the Giggle Club books you have read.

TEE HEE!

HA HA!

The Perfect Little Monster

Judy Hindley   illustrated by Jonathan Lycett-Smith

WALKER BOOKS
AND SUBSIDIARIES
LONDON · BOSTON · SYDNEY

Once there was a perfect little baby monster.
He had **horrible** little eyes and
a **horrible** little nose and
as soon as he was born,
he scowled.

His family loved him.

Baby Monster yelled and howled and made a **terrible** racket.

He threw his rattle and broke his bowl and made a **terrible** mess.

"Isn't he a perfect little monster!"
bragged his parents.

His sister taught him
how to **sneer**
and **snarl**.

His brother showed him
how to **bash** things
and **trash** things.

"Baby Monster learns so quickly!"
his parents said.

For his first birthday party, Baby Monster's proud parents invited all the monster aunts, and all the monster uncles and all the many **horrible** monster cousins.

Everyone gathered
around Baby Monster.
"Give us a great big scowl!"
said his mother
and father.

Baby Monster twitched his **horrible** little nose.

He screwed up his **horrible** little eyes.

He opened his
horrible
little
mouth

and stretched his
horrible
little
lips.

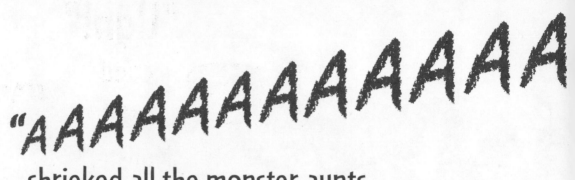

"AAAAAAAAAAAAA

shrieked all the monster aunts
and uncles and all the many
horrible monster cousins.

That perfect little baby monster ...

was smiling!

To Vanessa, for the vital spark
J. H.

For Audrey
J. L-S.

First published 2000 by Walker Books Ltd
87 Vauxhall Walk, London SE11 5HJ

10 9 8 7 6 5 4 3 2 1

Text © 2000 Judy Hindley
Illustrations © 2000 Jonathan Lycett-Smith

This book has been typeset in Cafeteria.

Printed in Hong Kong

British Library Cataloguing in Publication Data
A catalogue record for this book is
available from the British Library.

ISBN 0-7445-6145-0 (hb)
ISBN 0-7445-6943-5 (pb)